Cat vs Dog

T0318105

Written by Narinder Dhami

Illustrated by Russ Daff

Collins

1 A new home

"Are you *sure* your dog likes cats?" Milo asked
Lily doubtfully. Bailey was big and shaggy-haired,
and he was panting with excitement as he eyed
the cat basket in Milo's hand. Secretly, Milo thought
Bailey looked rather scary.

"Bailey *loves* cats!" Lily replied, glaring at Milo. She'd met him before, but she still wasn't convinced she liked him very much. And now Milo, his dad and their cat Pixie were moving in with Lily, her mum and Bailey. Lily couldn't help feeling anxious about it.

"They'll soon get used to each other," said Lily's mum, beaming at Milo's dad.

Milo hoped they wouldn't waste time chatting. He and his dad hadn't unpacked their stuff from the removal van yet, and Milo was worried his new bedroom wouldn't have space for all his things. His bedroom at home had been exactly the right size.

Milo screwed his eyes up, trying not to cry, and Lily was extremely annoyed.

Why is Milo pulling a horrible face? she thought. *He's so rude! I wish he wasn't moving in.*

"It's time Pixie and Bailey got acquainted," said Milo's dad, unfastening the cat basket.

Pixie strolled out of the cat basket, and Bailey barked a greeting. He lunged forward so forcefully that Lily lost her grip on his collar.

"Get away!" Milo yelled as Bailey bounded towards Pixie. The cat arched her back, hissing loudly, and leapt up onto the stair post out of reach.

Yowling indignantly, Pixie leant down and smacked Bailey's nose. Bailey yelped and scuttled away.

"Your cat hurt my dog!" Lily gasped.

"He shouldn't have chased Pixie!" Milo retorted.

"I thought Bailey loved cats?" Milo's dad whispered to Lily's mum.

"Oh dear," Lily's mum sighed. "That's a good start!"

2 Settling in

Milo gazed around his enormous bedroom and realised there was plenty of room for all his stuff. Carefully, he began placing books on the shelves.

Lily came out of her bedroom opposite Milo's.
"Why are you sorting all your books into alphabetical order?" she asked, open-mouthed with amazement.

"So I can find them easily," Milo snapped, wishing she'd leave him alone. He glanced curiously into Lily's bedroom and gasped with shock. The whole place appeared to have been turned upside down.

"Have we been burgled?" Milo asked nervously.

"Oh, very funny!" Lily snapped crossly.

Suddenly, there was a loud, mournful howl from downstairs.

"That's Bailey!" Lily gasped. "What's your cat done *now*?"

"Don't blame Pixie!" Milo said furiously.

They rushed downstairs and found Pixie snoozing peacefully in Bailey's enormous basket.

"Poor Bailey!" Lily said.

"Where's Pixie's food gone?" Milo wondered, staring at the bowl. "She always saves some for later."

Bailey licked his lips.

"Bailey ate Pixie's food!" Milo said accusingly.

"Good!" Lily retorted. "Pixie shouldn't have stolen his basket!"

Milo was so upset, he decided to have one of his favourite chocolate biscuits to cheer himself up. However, he was shocked to discover the biscuit tin was completely empty.

Milo dashed into the living room where Lily was watching TV.

"Did you eat all my favourite biscuits?" he demanded.

"Our parents said we had to share everything," Lily replied.

"But you *didn't* share!" Milo shouted. *"*You scoffed them *all!"*

"Lily?" Mum called from upstairs.

Lily stood up, and Milo immediately grabbed her chair.

"That's *my* favourite seat!" Lily yelled.

"We're supposed to share everything, remember?" Milo said.

3 Missing

It had been a long week. Lily sighed deeply, closing her bedroom door. She hated living with Milo. They'd argued constantly all week.

To Lily's surprise, Pixie was asleep in the sunshine on her bedroom windowsill.

"Hello, Puss," Lily said. Quickly, she cleared away some of the clutter so Pixie had more space.

Milo sat cross-legged on his bed, trying to read. He couldn't concentrate though because he was far too miserable.

The door burst open and Bailey ambled in. He leapt up onto the bed and settled down, resting his head on Milo's knee.

"Good dog," Milo said, very surprised.

Lily opened her bedroom door just as Milo
opened his. Purring, Pixie trotted up to Bailey and they
rubbed noses.

"Don't give Bailey chocolate," Lily said. "It makes
dogs sick."

"Don't forget Pixie isn't allowed outside yet,"
Milo warned. "She might get lost."

They retreated inside their separate bedrooms
and slammed the doors.

"Do you know where Pixie is, Dad?" Milo asked, the following afternoon. "I haven't seen her for ages."

"She might be asleep in Lily's bedroom," his dad replied.

Milo knocked at Lily's door, but there was no answer. He slipped inside and, to his horror, he noticed that the window was ajar.

Milo darted across the room, tripping over a pile of books. Leaning out of the window, he scanned the back garden, but Pixie had vanished.

"Why are you in my room?" Lily demanded accusingly.

Milo whirled round. "You left the window open on purpose!" he hollered. "Now Pixie's gone!"

Lily turned pale.

"I-I didn't do it on purpose!" she stammered. "I thought the window was too high for Pixie to escape."

"She could have jumped down onto the garden shed!" Milo yelled. "Look, it's right underneath the window!"

"I'm sorry!" Lily mumbled guiltily, but Milo had already disappeared.

4 Lost and found

Milo charged outside into the back garden, flinging doors open as he went.

"Pixie!" he yelled, his heart pounding with dread.

The garden appeared to be empty. Milo wrenched back the stiff bolts on the gate and then peered out into the street.

Dejected, Milo turned away. He was about to close the gate when his dad waved from Lily's bedroom window.

"Milo, Lily's found Pixie!"

"Yes!" Milo punched the air with delight and hurtled back through the garden into the kitchen.

Lily was cradling a dusty Pixie in her arms.

"I heard her yowling," Lily explained. "Somehow she'd managed to get herself locked in the attic."

"Thank you," Milo said, hugging Pixie tenderly. "And I'm sorry I said you left your window open on purpose."

"Bailey will be relieved that Pixie's safe and sound," Lily's mum remarked. "They've become good friends."

"Yes, they've learnt how to get along," Milo's dad agreed.

"Where *is* Bailey?" Lily wondered.

A cold feeling of dread swept over Milo, and the colour drained from his face.

"Bailey was there when I unbolted the garden gate!" Milo gasped, and immediately he sprinted out of the back door. Milo's feeling of dread increased when he saw the gate flapping open in the breeze, and no sign of Bailey.

"I forgot to shut the gate properly," Milo blurted out. "I'm *so* sorry, Lily."

5 A new beginning

Lily didn't say anything when Milo apologised, but he realised that was because she was struggling not to cry. Their parents were looking concerned, too. Milo hung his head, feeling very ashamed. This was completely his fault.

"Bailey can't have gone far," said Milo's dad, surveying the street. "Let's start searching."

Lily fought hard not to burst into sobs. She couldn't imagine what she'd do if Bailey was gone forever. He'd been a birthday gift from her dad.

They searched up and down the street, peering into gardens and behind parked cars.

They were nearing the end of the street when Milo heard a rustling sound among the trees.

"Bailey?" Milo called hopefully.

The rustling sound increased. Then a squirrel darted nervously out of the bushes.

Milo wondered if he'd frightened the squirrel. Or had the squirrel spotted something else?

"Bailey?" Milo shouted again. He was overwhelmed with sheer relief when the big, shaggy dog bounded out of the trees towards him.

Bailey wasn't alone. He was accompanied by a tiny, bedraggled white kitten that mewed pitifully at them.

"Look, Bailey's acquired a friend," said Milo's dad. "I wonder if it's a stray?"

Milo scooped the kitten up into his arms where it purred contentedly.

"If the kitten *is* a stray," he said thoughtfully, "can it stay with us and be mine and Lily's pet to share?"

"You're a genius, Milo!" Lily exclaimed, smiling at him.

Milo and Lily's letters

Hello, Mum,

Dad and I have moved in with Lily and her mum. I was really anxious at first because I could tell straightaway that Lily didn't want us there. *And* Bailey, Lily's dog, attacked Pixie!

Anyway, I've realised that Bailey's not scary, really. He's just boisterous.

Lily and I are avoiding each other. You'd laugh if you saw her bedroom – it looks like a hurricane hit it! I did notice though that she's got lots of books, just like me. But hers are on the floor, not the shelves!

Love, Milo

Hi, Dad!!!

Everything's really different here. Milo and his dad moved in a few days ago, and they brought their cat, Pixie. Bailey went MAD when he saw her, but he was just being friendly. Pixie's a bit snooty (just like Milo!) and she wouldn't let me touch her at first. But this afternoon I found her asleep on my bedroom windowsill, and she purred when I stroked her head. I suppose she's kind of cute (not like Milo, ha ha!).

Bailey sends lots of kisses and tail wags.

Love, Lily x

31

Ideas for reading

Written by Gill Matthews
Primary Literacy Consultant

Reading objectives:

- draw inferences such as inferring characters' feelings, thoughts and motives from their actions, and justifying inferences with evidence
- predict what might happen from details stated and implied
- identify how language, structure and presentation contribute to meaning

Spoken language objectives:

- articulate and justify answers, arguments and opinions
- use spoken language to develop understanding through speculating, hypothesising, imagining and exploring ideas

Curriculum links: Relationships education – Families and people who care for me; Caring friendships

Interest words: glaring, beaming, gasped, retorted

Build a context for reading

- Ask children to look at the front cover illustration. Discuss how they think the boy and girl feel about each other, explaining their reasons.
- Read the title and check children's understanding of *vs* (shortened version of *versus*). Explore how they think the cat and dog feel about each other.
- Read the back-cover blurb. This is a situation that may be familiar to some of the children. Sensitively explore why the children think Milo and Lily aren't happy.
- Check whether any of the children have both a dog and a cat. Ask how they get on with each other.

Understand and apply reading strategies

- Read Chapter 1 aloud to the children. Ask questions that explore the characters' feelings in order to develop children's inferential skills, e.g. *Why do you think Lily is feeling anxious about Milo and his dad moving in? Why do you think Milo tries not to cry?*
- Discuss how the children think everyone is going to get on – including Bailey and Pixie.